Ken, Lily and Lady Lia

Om KIDZ

An imprint of Om Books International

Om KIDZ | Om Books International

Reprinted in 2023

Corporate & Editorial Office
A-12, Sector 64, Noida 201 301
Uttar Pradesh, India
Phone: +91 120 477 4100
Email: editorial@ombooks.com
Website: www.ombooksinternational.com

ISBN: 978-93-52760-28-2

Printed in India

10 9 8 7 6 5 4 3 2

Sales Office
107, Ansari Road, Darya Ganj
New Delhi 110 002, India
Phone: +91 11 4000 9000
Email: sales@ombooks.com
Website: www.ombooks.com

Ken, Lily and Lady Lia

Paste your photograph here

My name is

In a **land** not very far away,
live Lily and **Ken**.

Lily is a **kind** girl. Her **little** brother **Ken** is a naughty boy.

They both **live** in a **large** house.

Ken calls himself the **king** of the house. This makes **Lily laugh.**

Ken is upset that his sister **laughs** at him.

He wants to teach her a **lesson.**

Lily has a **little** doll

named **Lady Lia.**

Lady Lia wears a

pretty, **light** pink dress.

Lily keeps her in her room.

Lily loves her doll very much.

Ken goes into **Lily's** room and **leaves** with **Lady Lia.**

He is sure that his sister will **learn** her **lesson** soon.

A few minutes **later, Lily looks** for her doll but can't find it. She thinks she **lost** it. She wonders where she **left** it.

Lily feels **lonely** without her **little** doll. **Ken locks** the doll in his room with a **key.**

He puts the **key** under the **lamp** in the **kitchen.**

Lily looks sad. She stays in her room and **listens** to music. Naughty **Ken** dances about. Now **Lily** will not **laugh** at him.

While dancing, **Ken** runs into the table.

He **loses** his balance and falls down. His foot is hurt.

Ken's foot hurts a **lot.** His **lips** begin to tremble. He starts to cry. **Lily** comes running to **Ken.**

Lily makes **Ken** sit on the sofa**. Ken** cries as she puts medicine on his foot.

Soon his pain becomes **less.**

Ken feels sorry.He **knows** his sister **loves** him a **lot.** At last, he gives the **key** to **Lily.** He **lets** her have **Lady Lia** again.

Lily is very happy to get her **Lady Lia** back. She hugs **Ken.** They have fun together.

Know your words

Naming words

land
Lily
lesson
lady
Lia
lamp
lips
lap
Ken
king
key
kitchen

Describing words

little
large
light
lonely
lot
less
later
last

Doing words

laugh
live
loves
learn
looks
lost
listens
loses
lets
locks
leaves
keeps
knows
kind

Sight words

left

Join the dots to show what Lily loves to play with. Colour it.

Help Ken reach Lily without running into any chairs.

Spot 5 differences in these two images.